The Whodunit Detective Agency

The Diamond Mystery

GROSSET & DUNLAP
Published by the Penguin Group
Penguin Group (USA) LLC, 375 Hudson Street, New York, New York 10014, USA

USA | Canada | UK | Ireland | Australia | New Zealand | India | South Africa | China

penguin.com
A Penguin Random House Company

Original title: LasseMajas Detektivbyrå: Diamantmysteriet
Text by Martin Widmark
Original cover and illustrations by Helena Willis

English language edition copyright © 2014 Penguin Group (USA) LLC. Original edition
published by Bonnier Carlsen Bokförlag, Sweden, 2002. Text copyright © 2002 by Martin
Widmark. Illustrations copyright © 2002 by Helena Willis. Published in 2014 by Grosset
& Dunlap, a division of Penguin Young Readers Group, 345 Hudson Street, New York,
New York 10014. GROSSET & DUNLAP is a trademark of Penguin Group (USA) LLC.
Manufactured in China.

Library of Congress Cataloging-in-Publication Data is available.

ISBN 978-0-448-48066-4 (pbk)   10 9 8 7
ISBN 978-0-448-48067-1 (hc)   10 9 8 7 6 5 4 3 2 1

The Whodunit Detective Agency

The Diamond Mystery

Martin Widmark
illustrated by Helena Willis

Grosset & Dunlap
An Imprint of Penguin Group (USA) LLC

The Diamond Mystery

The books in *The Whodunit Detective Agency* series are set in the charming little town of Pleasant Valley. It's the sort of close-knit community where nearly everyone knows one another. The town and characters are all fictional, of course . . . or are they?

The main characters, Jerry and Maya, are classmates and close friends who run a small detective agency together.

CHAPTER 1

The Detectives' Office

The streets were empty in the little town of Pleasant Valley. At three thirty on a chilly February afternoon it was already growing dark. A late winter storm had left the town slick with freezing rain.

There was a light shining through the basement window of a small house just east of town. Inside, two children enjoyed the cozy warmth of the basement. Their names were Jerry and Maya, classmates and good friends from school.

They were off from school for winter break. Most of their friends were charging down the sledding hill, but neither Jerry nor Maya felt like joining them. They had something else on their minds.

"I have a feeling that something exciting is going to happen soon," said Jerry hopefully.

"Mmm-hmm," mumbled Maya. She had her nose in a book as usual.

The two classmates had set up a small office in Maya's basement, and they sat in two old armchairs that stood next to a table piled high with books. More volumes of thick books—Maya's dad's detective stories—lined the walls. Maya and Jerry liked to sit in this room and read. During winter break they wanted to learn everything about how thieves and police officers worked.

You see, Maya and Jerry were not just

friends: They were partners as well. Together, they ran a detective agency: the Whodunit Detective Agency.

A detective, of course, is a type of police officer who wears regular clothes instead of an official uniform. A detective carries out investigations and spies on suspects, takes photographs and looks through binoculars. In the end, a good detective solves the case and catches the criminal.

THE WHODUNIT DETECTIVE AGENCY EQUIPMENT

1 CAMERA WITH A FLASH

2 BINOCULARS

3 MAGNIFYING GLASS

4 MIRROR

5 FALSE NOSES AND WIGS

6 FLASHLIGHT

7 SAFE

"I wish we had a really exciting case," said Maya with a sigh.

"Maybe all of the thieves are on winter break, too," said Jerry.

Maya opened a tidy cabinet to make sure everything inside was well organized. It held everything they needed for their detective work:

1 A camera with a flash—to take photos in the dark.

2 A pair of binoculars—to spy on things from far away.

3 A magnifying glass—to check for fingerprints.

4 A mirror—to peer around corners.

5 Several false noses and wigs—to disguise themselves.

6 A few flashlights—to use when it was dark.

7 A safe—to protect the money they'd earned.

But their safe was empty, because nothing exciting had happened for a long time. But once it did, Jerry and Maya were ready: They had put up signs all around Pleasant Valley. On nearly every streetlight and door they had hung posters that said:

The Whodunit Detective Agency
Now accepting exciting and dangerous assignments.
Lost wallets and runaway cats recovered.
Low prices, tax included.

So, while Jerry and Maya waited for an exciting case, they researched detective stories. Maya was just about to fill Jerry in on the book she was reading: It was a story about a dognapper who stole dogs tied up outside stores and then called the dogs' owners to demand ransoms for the poor pooches. Maya was upset just thinking about it. That was one criminal she would really like to catch!

But before she had a chance to describe the case to Jerry, there was a knock on the door. Jerry and Maya looked at each other in surprise. Who could it be?

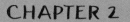

CHAPTER 2

A Desperate Man Seeks Help

Before Maya could move an inch, Jerry leaped up, ran up the stairs, and opened the front door. Standing on the steps was a man with a bushy black mustache wearing a striped wool hat and wet shoes.

It was Mohammed Carat, the richest man in all of Pleasant Valley.

Mohammed Carat owned the jeweler's store on Church Street. His store was famous all across the country—from New York to Los Angeles—for its spectacular diamonds, rings, earrings, and other fancy jewelry. What could the jeweler possibly want with Jerry and Maya?

Jerry showed Mr. Carat down to their

small office in the basement.

"Welcome, Mr. Carat. Please sit down," said Maya, gesturing toward an empty chair.

Mohammed Carat plunked down in the armchair and removed a handkerchief from his coat pocket. He was sweating, and Jerry and Maya could see that he was nervous.

"What can we do for you, Mr. Carat?" asked Jerry politely.

"I'm desperate, just desperate for help!" began Mohammed Carat. "I saw your poster on the streetlight outside my store. Are you still accepting cases?"

Maya and Jerry nodded and eagerly took out their pens and notebooks.

"As you probably know, I've owned the jewelry store on Church Street for many years, and business has been booming," started Mohammed Carat. "People come to my quiet little store here in Pleasant

Valley from far and wide. But now it seems my luck has run out," he said, and blew his nose into the handkerchief.

"What do you mean?" asked Jerry.

"My trust has been violated, that's what I mean!" exclaimed Mohammed Carat. "One of the people working in my store is stealing my diamonds. I'm sure of it! In the past month, five extremely valuable gems have disappeared, and I have no idea how. I am a very cautious man: I require everyone who works in the store to empty their bags and pockets before they go home, but I never find anything. Nothing has been carried out of the store—I'm absolutely certain of that."

"What do the police think?" asked Maya.

"The police have been investigating and keeping watch since the very first diamond disappeared, but they don't have a suspect. They said they can't do anything until the thief makes a mistake and gives himself or herself away."

Mohammed loosened the tie around his neck.

"Soon, I'll be ruined and will have to close my store." He sniffed. "Without my famous diamonds, my customers will quickly lose interest in my jewelry store altogether."

Jerry and Maya could see that Mr. Carat was really upset.

"This is a tricky situation," said Jerry, scratching his nose with his pen. That helped him think. "The police can't do any more to help, and they don't have a suspect. Is that right?"

"Absolutely right," replied Mohammed Carat. "But, I have an idea: I'll hire the two of you to work in my store. While you're working, you can secretly keep an eye on the employees and tip me off to any suspicious behavior. You can help me find out who has been stealing my diamonds! Are you interested? Please say you are!"

Maya and Jerry exchanged a quick glance. "We'll start tomorrow."

CHAPTER 3

The Investigation Begins

The next day, the sun was shining brightly. Maya and Jerry each packed a bag containing their detective kits and took the bus to Church Street. They got off in front of the hotel, just down the road from Mohammed Carat's famous jewelry store between the café and the post office.

Jerry and Maya walked to the old church so they could get a look at the store from across the street. The store was at street level, and Mr. Carat owned the two floors above it.

"So, there's a diamond thief in there somewhere," said Jerry. "Are you scared?"

"Oh, come on! Let's get started," scoffed Maya, dragging Jerry toward the store.

They crossed the street and opened the

front door. A bell chimed as they went in. Maya looked around carefully. An elderly assistant asked if she could help them. When Maya asked to speak to the owner, the assistant led the two detectives to an office at the back of the store.

The assistant knocked on the door to the office.

"Come in," they heard Mohammed Carat call.

Maya opened the door, and Mohammed Carat stood up from behind his desk. He walked toward them with his arms outstretched.

"I'm so glad to see you!" he cried.

Then he lowered his voice and whispered, "Another diamond disappeared yesterday; that's the sixth. I can't understand how they do it! I need your help more than ever."

Jerry noticed the elderly woman lingering in the doorway. She seemed to be listening curiously.

"You may go back to the front, Vivian," said Mohammed Carat, shutting the door behind her.

"Let's get started," said Jerry as they settled down on a big brown sofa. "Could you tell us about the people who work here, and what a typical day in the store is like?"

Mohammed Carat took out his handkerchief and blew his nose loudly. He walked to his desk, opened one of the drawers, and took out a few photos.

"The store opens at 10:00 a.m. and closes at 6:00 p.m. At some point during that time, a diamond disappears. The whole thing is impossible to explain. I'm going mad!" he yelled.

"Um, Mr. Carat, please try to calm down," said Maya.

"Excuse me," Mr. Carat said as he collected himself. "Other than myself, there are three people who work here."

Mohammed Carat passed one of the photos to Jerry and Maya.

"Vivian Leander, store assistant. You've already met her—she's the one who showed you to my office. Vivian works in the front of the store and helps the customers. She's been with the business for many years and has always done an excellent job.

"But she ran into some trouble last year. Her house burned down, and I believe the insurance company is refusing to pay her any money," explained Mohammed Carat. "Apparently, Vivian was behind on home

insurance payments, so now she's short
on cash. Just last week, she came into my
office and asked for a raise. I would be
happy to help her, but, as I am sure you can
understand, there's no way I can afford a
raise now."

Jerry scratched his nose with his pen and
made a note in his notebook:

Suspect's motive: Vivian
Leander needs money.

Mohammed Carat passed them another
photo.

"Danny Braveheart works on the second floor, just above the store," he continued. "He cleans and polishes the jewelry before it's sold. To be honest, Danny is a bit grumpy for my taste, but he's always on time and keeps things in order. He is a trustworthy employee.

"Danny's dad actually owned this store years and years ago," Mohammed Carat went on. "But he had financial problems and had to sell it. That's when I bought the store. Otherwise, Danny would be the boss here today."

Jerry didn't have to scratch his nose this time. He simply wrote:

Suspect's motive: Danny Braveheart wants to take over the store.

Mohammed Carat passed Jerry and Maya the third and final photo.

"Luke Smith works on the top floor of the building. He cuts diamonds and sets them into elegant rings and necklaces. Luke hasn't worked here very long, but he's careful and very good at his job. He's worked in the jewelry business for many years, and his previous employers were very pleased with him. Luke likes nice clothes and fast sports cars. He bought a new car just last week, actually."

Mohammed Carat laughed. "You should have seen Danny Braveheart's face when Luke showed off his new car. Danny looked at the car with disgust and then at Luke with loathing. 'Three hundred eighty horsepower,' Luke had bragged and patted the hood. To which Danny had replied, 'You only need one horsepower if you choose the right one' and stormed off.

"None of us—Vivian, Luke, nor I—understood what he meant," continued Mohammed Carat. "Danny was definitely in one of his grumpy moods. But like I said, Luke Smith is a nice guy. He's into fitness: He's always going for a jog and carrying around an apple to snack on."

Jerry wrote in his notebook:

Luke Smith has plenty of money. Where does it come from?

"All right, then! I think that's all you need to know," said Mohammed Carat as he sprang up from the sofa. "Now I'll introduce you to the staff."

CHAPTER 4

The Suspects

In the hallway between the office and the store, Mr. Carat stopped suddenly and lowered his voice to a whisper.

"Please help me catch the thief. Otherwise, I'll be bankrupt soon."

Jerry and Maya had no time to reply before Mohammed Carat walked on. They followed him into the store to meet the other three employees: Vivian Leander, Danny Braveheart, and Luke Smith. Mohammed Carat stood in the middle of the store and introduced everyone.

"This is Jerry and Maya. They're going to work here for a few days. They will wash the windows, empty the trash, run errands, and help with other odds and ends."

Vivian and Luke stepped forward to shake hands and say hello. Vivian wore a glittering necklace.

Strange, thought Jerry. *She's supposed to be short on money.*

Vivian Leander smiled at Jerry and Maya, but they sensed her mind was on something else. *Why did she stop and listen outside the owner's door earlier? How could she afford such an expensive gold necklace? What does she know about the stolen diamonds?*

Luke held a bright green apple in his hand and laughed, showing his big white teeth. *He likes fruit,* Maya remembered Mohammed Carat saying.

"An apple a day keeps the doctor away," said Luke with a laugh, patting his well-toned stomach.

Then he threw the apple up in the air and tried to catch it behind his back. But he missed, and the apple fell with a thud and rolled under the glass cabinet near Vivian Leander.

She turned up her nose at Luke, who was down on his knees, digging around under the cabinet.

Danny Braveheart smiled sourly at Luke Smith, who he thought was making a fool of himself, scrambling around on the floor. Danny did not step forward to say hello like the others. He stayed in his corner and glared at the two children. He didn't seem to like anyone new coming into the store.

"All right, then! Let's get back to work," said Mr. Carat, clapping his hands together. "Time is money, as we all know."

Maya immediately headed to the broom closet and took out a bucket, cloth, and squeegee. She started cleaning the store window while keeping her eyes and ears alert.

Back on her side of the store, Vivian Leander started to hum and fiddle around behind the counter.

Before too long, the first customer of the day came in. It was an elderly gentleman with a gray mustache and a hat. He entered the store like a man on a mission.

He stopped in front of a glass display case containing a selection of expensive diamond necklaces.

He must be looking for something beautiful for the woman he loves, thought Maya.

As soon as she saw their first customer, Vivian Leander blushed and fluttered around nervously.

Since Maya had the inside situation under control, Jerry left the store to investigate outside. He hung his binoculars around his neck and jogged across the street to the church. Inside, he met the church caretaker. Jerry introduced himself as a local ornithologist.

"A local orni . . . what?" asked the caretaker.

"An ornithologist. It means bird-watcher," explained Jerry. "Someone who studies birds.

"I was wondering if I could do a bit of bird-watching from the church tower," he continued, holding up his binoculars. "There have been reports of a South American Jacuzzi Stork here in town—a very rare bird. If I am lucky enough to have a sighting of it, I'll report it to the newspaper right away. It would be a huge sensation for Pleasant Valley."

"I'm sure that'll be all right," replied the caretaker, and showed Jerry the door leading up to the tower.

Up in the tower, the caretaker opened some of the shutters that faced the street. He wished Jerry luck and headed back downstairs.

Once alone, Jerry crouched down

and began looking through his binoculars at Mohammed Carat's jewelry store on the opposite side of the street. The investigation was on!

CHAPTER 5

Investigations Inside and Out

Down in the store, Jerry could see Vivian Leander showing jewelry to the elderly gentleman. The tray lined with red velvet held glittering necklaces and sparkling rings. *She looks pretty happy*, thought Jerry. *I wonder why?*

The elderly man looked at the jewelry, but he seemed more interested in the assistant.

Jerry could see Maya cleaning on the other side of the store. He was sure she was trying to hear what Vivian and the customer were saying.

When the elderly gentleman turned to leave, Vivian stopped him with a kiss on the nose! What service!

Does she do that to all the customers?
wondered Jerry.

Inside the store, Maya took her window-cleaning supplies and headed up to the second floor. She knocked and then opened the door to Danny Braveheart's office.

"I'm going to clean the windows in here," she said politely.

Danny Braveheart quickly shut something away in his desk drawer—something he obviously didn't want Maya to see. Maya tried to peer across the room to see what it might be, but Danny stopped her with a hiss. "Don't you have something else to do besides snoop on me? Go ahead and start cleaning the windows if you must!"

What a nasty guy, thought Maya. *He's definitely hiding something.*

From his perch in the church tower, Jerry could see everything. Maya had moved to the window. She cautiously waved to him and he waved back. But then Jerry saw something else—something that scared him.

Danny Braveheart had opened his desk drawer and taken out a long knife! He tested the blade against his thumb and nodded approvingly.

Maya is trapped in a room with a mad man wielding a knife, and I can't do anything about it! Jerry thought desperately.

He waved frantically at Maya and gestured for her to turn around. But Maya just waved happily back.

R-I-I-I-P!

Maya spun around at the sudden noise, and saw Danny Braveheart opening letters with a long, sharp knife. It was a letter opener.

"I've finished the windows in here," said Maya nervously.

Danny Braveheart didn't answer. When Maya left the room, she heard him opening the desk drawer again.

I guess he's taking out whatever he hid before, thought Maya.

Jerry lowered his binoculars and breathed a huge sigh of relief.

No one said detective work was easy, he thought. Then he heard someone stomping up the stairs to the church tower.

It was the caretaker again.

"Have you seen a Jacuzzi Stork yet?" he asked curiously.

"Not yet," answered Jerry. "But an ornithologist needs a lot of patience. Jacuzzi Storks are tough to spot this early in the year."

"If the newspaper decides to write anything about the bird, could you tell them that I was the one who opened the church tower for you?" asked the caretaker.

"Of course!" said Jerry.

"My name is Roland Sussman—Sussman with three Ss," said the caretaker.

But Jerry hadn't heard him because he was already busy looking through the binoculars again.

CHAPTER 6

The Missing Apple

Maya was now on the top floor, standing just outside Luke Smith's office. She took a deep breath and lifted her hand to knock. After finding a large knife on the second floor she wondered what she might find on the third floor. Suddenly, the door opened and Maya was confronted by Luke Smith dressed in a tracksuit. Maya gasped.

"Sorry to surprise you," Luke said kindly. "I always go for a jog before lunch." He gestured to his sneakers and smiled.

Through his binoculars, Jerry could see Maya's surprised expression. Then he saw Luke Smith leave the building through the front door.

Luke Smith
ran a few short
feet, then
stopped by
the building's
drainpipe,
kneeling down to
tie his shoelaces.
With a quick
motion, he
picked up
something
from the street,
hopped up, and ran
off toward the post
office. He had a big
smile on his face.

*That's a strange
route for a jog,
thought Jerry.*

Meanwhile, Maya looked around Luke's office. It had the same layout as Danny Braveheart's office below. There was one workbench and two windows facing the street—one of which was open.

Luke's tools were spread out along the workbench, and some of his clothes hung on the coatrack against the wall.

Maya walked to the open window and waved to Jerry in the church tower. Jerry waved back.

Maya moved around the room slowly, looking for something without knowing exactly what she was looking for. She picked up the tools, twisting and turning them to see how they worked. She checked the drawers in the desk: They were locked.

There's something missing, she thought.

Then she realized: *The apple!*

Something told her that Luke's green apple was very important. She didn't know why; it was just a feeling she had. When she pictured Luke, she immediately saw the green apple right in front of her eyes.

She looked everywhere but couldn't find the apple. *He must have eaten it,* she thought, *and I know just how to find out!* Maya raced over to the trash can to look for the apple core—but it was empty!

Suddenly, Jerry saw Luke Smith leave the post office. He tucked a small key in his pocket and jogged back to the jewelry store.

Oh no! Maya was still nosing around his office looking for clues!

Jerry watched Luke open the jewelry store door and disappear into the building. *This is where a good tip-off would come in handy,* thought Jerry. He needed to warn

Maya somehow.
Jerry opened his
detective bag and
took out a small
mirror. He held it out
through the shutters
of the church tower
and turned it toward the sun.
It caught a ray of sunshine and reflected
straight into Luke Smith's workshop.

Jerry directed the beam of light into
Maya's face.

At first, Maya was irritated and held
her hands across her eyes—but then she
understood that Jerry was trying to tell her

something. She ran across the room to the cleaning supplies and pretended to work.

Just in time! As soon as she picked up the bucket and squeegee, the door to the room opened. In walked a still-smiling Luke Smith.

"Hi there, junior worker," he said with a smile.

"I've just finished the window," Maya said cheerfully, and headed out the door.

Phew, that was a little close for comfort. Jerry sighed over in the church tower.

CHAPTER 7

A Snack and a Solution

On the way down from Luke Smith's room, Maya bumped into Danny Braveheart, and he dropped what he was carrying. Betting slips and gambling tickets fell like confetti and scattered down the stairs. Danny hastily gathered all of the fallen paperwork and cast a worried look down the stairs.

Aha! thought Maya. *That's what he was doing when I interrupted him earlier: He was sitting at his desk gambling* instead of polishing the jewelry like he's supposed to. *And now he's afraid that Mohammed Carat will catch him.*

"Look where you're going, you clumsy fool," barked Danny Braveheart before disappearing into his room.

Maya quickly excused herself and continued down the stairs.

Jerry came down from the church tower. In the church, he ran into Roland Sussman, the man with three Ss.

"Did you spot any birds?" asked the caretaker.

"No, no luck today," replied Jerry, shaking his head. He said good-bye and walked across the street.

Jerry and Maya had arranged to meet at the café next to the jeweler's. There, they each ordered apple juice and a granola bar.

They took a seat in the corner of the café where they could talk without being overheard. It had been a long, difficult day, and it wasn't over yet!

It was time for the two detectives to discuss what they had each seen and heard that day.

They sat in the café for an hour, talking and comparing notes. Jerry saw a lot that Maya couldn't have, and Maya filled him

in on what she heard while she was working in the store. The two of them put together what they knew, and the clues fit together like the pieces of a puzzle.

The waitress was surprised when she checked on the two children: They had barely touched their food!

After a while, Jerry and Maya nodded at each other with satisfaction and got up from the table. All of the pieces were in place and they knew who the thief was!

Jerry and Maya entered the jewelry store and walked toward Mohammed Carat's office. They knocked, but nobody answered. Strange . . . where could he be? Carefully, Maya nudged the door. It wasn't locked, so Maya gently pushed it open. Inside, they found Mohammed Carat lying on his back on the brown sofa. He wasn't moving! Was he dead?

Jerry and Maya rushed over.

Thankfully, he wasn't dead—he was breathing. But he was lying completely still, staring blankly ahead. *He must be in shock,* thought Jerry. The two detectives saw tears running down Mr. Carat's cheeks. They dripped to the floor, where his earlier tears had already begun to form a little puddle.

"Today, a seventh diamond was stolen," he sniffled. "It's over! I will have to sell my beloved store."

"Not so fast, Mr. Carat," said Maya. "We think we know who has stolen your diamonds."

In a flash, Mohammed Carat sat up on the sofa, his eyes wide.

CHAPTER 8

Who, Why, and How?

"Let me guess," said Mohammed Carat eagerly, wiping tears from his mustache. "It must be Vivian! She's disappointed because she's not getting a raise. She stole my diamonds so she could build a new house, and then she buys expensive necklaces and clothes with the money instead. Oh, how could she?!" groaned Mohammed Carat.

"Vivian is innocent," said Maya. "But she has a fiancé—a rich man who showers her with presents. Vivian didn't steal your diamonds. The only thing she's guilty of is kissing customers at work."

"I know who it is!" cried Mohammed Carat, jumping up. "It's Danny Braveheart. That crafty old fox! He's cheated me."

Mohammed Carat shook his clenched fist toward the floor above, where Danny Braveheart worked.

"He stole my diamonds to ruin me!" roared Mohammed Carat. "Once he has enough money, he'll buy back the store that his father once owned."

"Of course Danny Braveheart wants to get rich," agreed Jerry. "But not by stealing your diamonds: He gambles on horse races. Danny Braveheart isn't a particularly friendly or dedicated employee, but he isn't a diamond thief."

Mohammed Carat sank to his knees. Weeping with rage, he banged his fists on the floor.

"Luke Smith!" he hollered. "You bragging, sports-car-driving villain! How could you?"

Mohammed Carat fell silent. A wrinkle appeared on his sweaty forehead.

"Yes . . . *how* could he?" he asked, and

looked at Jerry and Maya. "How on earth did he get the diamonds out of the store, and where is he hiding them?"

"The main character in this story is actually an apple," said Maya. "An apple that *isn't* there."

Mohammed Carat scratched his head. Jerry scratched his nose. Mr. Carat clearly didn't understand, so Maya continued.

"Every morning, Luke Smith brings an apple to the office. But he doesn't eat it, and he doesn't take it home. So the question is: Where does the apple go?"

"Yes," Jerry added. "In the mornings, Luke works alone in his room. And that's when he takes the opportunity to press one of

1. Luke throws the apple out the window.

2. The apple rolls into the gutter.

3. The apple falls into the drainpi[pe]

4. The apple rolls onto the sidewa[lk]

5. Luke picks up th[e] apple.

6. Luke jogs to the post office.

your diamonds into his green apple. Then he opens the window and tosses the apple onto the roof. The apple rolls across the roof and into the gutter, where it then falls down the drainpipe and onto the sidewalk below. As soon as that's taken care of, Luke puts on his tracksuit and goes for his daily jog."

Mohammed Carat looked at the two sleuths with his mouth wide open. Maya said, "Just in front of the drainpipe, Luke, your healthy, apple-eating jogger, stops and pretends to tie his shoelaces. That's when he picks up the diamond-stuffed apple and runs to the post office to lock it in a safe-deposit box."

"We think there will be seven green—or not-so-green—apples in the safe-deposit box, and you'll find the key in Luke Smith's tracksuit," concluded Maya.

"By golly! You've solved the case!" cheered Mohammed Carat as he jumped up in the air with joy. After he calmed down, he went to his safe and took out a thick stack of dollar bills.

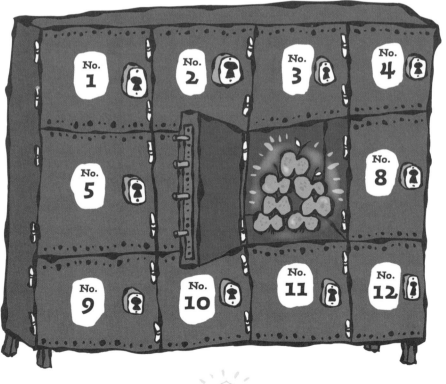

"Here you are!" he said happily. "I am very pleased with the Whodunit Detective Agency! But now, you must excuse me: Luke Smith and I are going to take a little walk to the post office together."

Jerry and Maya walked out of the office. Vivian Leander was standing outside. She had been listening at the door as usual.

"Oh, I was just . . . ," she said, blushing.

Jerry and Maya looked at each other and tried to hide their smiles.

On the bus ride home, Maya suggested they buy a computer with the money they had just earned from Mohammed Carat. But Jerry wasn't listening. He was looking out the window and scratching his nose.

"Now I understand," he said finally, and laughed. "Danny Braveheart was talking about gambling on horses when he said, 'You only need one horsepower if you choose the right one.'"

"Exactly!" exclaimed Maya. "He was thinking about winning a horse race, as usual.

"A good detective leaves no questions unanswered," she said, and smiled admiringly at Jerry.

The next day, the church caretaker, Roland Sussman, and everyone else in the little town read something very exciting in the newspaper:

THE WHODUNIT AGENCY SOLVES YET ANOTHER CASE

The young detectives of The Whodunit Detective Agency, Maya and Jerry, have successfully solved a difficult case. Through clever investigative work, they have linked one of Mohammed Carat's jewelry-store employees to a crime.

Twenty-nine-year-old Luke Smith has confessed to police that he had stolen seven diamonds, each worth thousands of dollars. Mysteriously, Jerry has told the paper that he and Maya have three Ss to thank for helping them solve the case.

Now, a long prison sentence awaits Luke Smith. And there will certainly be many more assignments to come for Jerry and Maya's newly opened, but already successful, detective agency.

Be sure to pick up

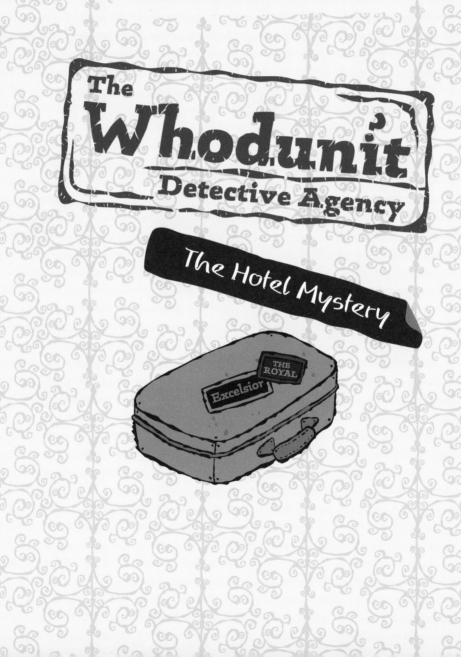

The **Whodunit?** Detective Agency

The Hotel Mystery

THE ROYAL
Excelsior

VIP Guests

Here in the meeting, the moody receptionist noisily drummed his fingers on the table. Clearly, he didn't think he had time to sit there.

Next to the unpleasant Bert Anderson sat his complete opposite: the friendly and always-cheerful Rita Henderson, a chef from New Orleans. Jerry's uncle said that the manager, Ronnie Hazelwood, had a crush on Rita.

Rita dreamed of one day opening her own restaurant in France. But she didn't have enough money, and spent most of her paychecks on lottery tickets and scratch cards, hoping to win big. During the meeting, she was scratching a card with a penny.

"Useless!" She laughed and ruffled Jerry's hair. "I didn't even win a dollar! But one day I'll hit the jackpot, and then I'll be off to France!"

Opposite friendly Rita sat Pierre Chalottes, a dark-haired and sad-looking housekeeper from France. Pierre didn't say much, but Jerry and Maya had noticed how he and Rita liked to sit together and whisper during their lunch breaks.

"Well, now," said Ronnie Hazelwood. "The hotel's holiday celebrations are under way." The manager's whole face lit up with a smile. "Maya is helping Rita bake a big gingerbread house, which will go in reception. First thing tomorrow morning, Jerry will decorate the tree in the lounge. We'll hand out the holiday presents there at 4:00 p.m. I'll dress up as Santa Claus—or do you think we should have

a reindeer this year? That could be a part for you, Bert!"

The hotel manager chuckled and gave Bert a friendly thump on the back. Maya saw Bert's upper lip twitch slightly. Some might have thought it was the beginning of a smile, but Maya suspected it was more of a snarl, and that Bert Anderson would like to bite his boss's hand.

"Anyway," the hotel manager continued, without noticing his receptionist's annoyance, "tomorrow is not only Christmas Eve, but also a very important day for the hotel. The Braeburn family has reserved the hotel's best suite. The family plans to stay for quite a while. This means a lot of money for the hotel, and goodness knows we certainly need it. We all must make sure that everything runs perfectly during their stay."

Jerry and Maya could see that the manager was nervous.

"Mr. and Mrs. Braeburn will be here with their daughter, Pippin, and a small dog, Winston."

The manager continued talking about the wealthy family: "Mr. Braeburn made it very clear that Winston is to receive the best treatment. Otherwise he could become stressed and stop eating. Evidently, the Braeburns own a very expensive and unusual dog, and nothing bad must happen to it," he firmly concluded.

"I'm sure everything will be fine with the dog. You'll see," Rita said with a laugh.

The hotel manager relaxed a little and gazed affectionately at Rita.

"Well, I think that covers everything," he said, and closed the meeting.

Then the staff members left the room and continued their preparations for the holiday celebrations.